HENRY
and the Dragon

After Henry Rabbit's father reads him a story about a fierce and frightening dragon, Henry is afraid that one of the creatures may live near his house. The shadow on his bedroom wall looks a lot like a dragon.

"What an imagination you have," Henry's father says. But Henry is sure there's a dragon somewhere, and he's determined to catch it.

After a mishap with his home-made dragon trap, Henry is sent to his room, where the dragon's shadow still lurks on the wall. Henry finally unearths the source of the scary shadow—and discovers that grownups sometimes aren't any braver than children.

Readers who enjoyed *Henry and the Red Stripes* will want to continue following Henry Rabbit on his adventurous journey through bunnyhood.

TO ROSA
in memory of Al

Clarion Books
Ticknor & Fields, a Houghton Mifflin Company

Copyright © 1984 by Eileen Christelow
All rights reserved. Printed in the U.S.A.

Library of Congress Cataloging in Publication Data

Christelow, Eileen.
Henry and the dragon.

Summary: At bedtime Henry Rabbit is sure he sees
the shadow of a dragon on his bedroom wall even though
his parents can find no evidence of it.
[Bedtime—Fiction. 2. Night—Fiction. 3. Fear
—Fiction. 4. Rabbits—Fiction] I. Title.
PZ7.C4523Hdr 1984   [E]   83-14405
ISBN 0-89919-220-3

Y   10 9 8 7 6 5 4 3 2 1

HENRY
and the Dragon

Eileen Christelow

Clarion Books

TICKNOR & FIELDS: A HOUGHTON MIFFLIN COMPANY

New York

One night Henry Rabbit's father read him a bedtime story about a fierce and frightening dragon.

When the story was finished Henry asked, "Do any dragons live near our house?"

"You don't need to worry," said Henry's father.
"Dragons are only make-believe."

He gave Henry a goodnight hug and a kiss, tucked
him into bed, and turned out the light.

"But there *might* be a dragon living near our house,"
Henry said to himself as he tried to fall asleep.
Then Henry noticed a shadow on his bedroom wall
that looked a little like a dragon.

And he heard a rustling noise outside his window.

"There might be a dragon outside our house right now!" whispered Henry.

He ran to tell his parents.

"There's a dragon somewhere around here!" he shouted. "I saw his shadow and I heard him moving about."

"What an imagination you have," said his father.

"There's no such thing as a dragon," said his mother. "Dragons are only make-believe."

Henry wanted his parents to look for the dragon anyway.

Henry's mother looked outside. She could not
find any dragons.

Henry's father turned on Henry's bedroom light.
He looked around the bedroom. He could not find
any dragons, either.

"I know there is a dragon somewhere," said Henry.

That night Henry decided that he would sleep better
in his parents' bed.

The next morning Henry buckled his wooden
sword around his waist.

He found a big ball of twine,

and he went outside to build a dragon trap.

He worked all day.

That night, when Henry went to bed, he tucked
his wooden sword under his pillow. He tried to sleep,
but he couldn't help noticing a shadow on his bedroom
wall that looked a little like a dragon.

And he couldn't help hearing a rustling
noise in the bushes.

Henry ran to tell his parents.
"I heard the dragon again!" he shouted.
"I saw his shadow! He's outside my window
right now!"

"Not again!" Henry's parents said.

But his father went outside to look behind the bushes anyway.

"Be very careful," whispered Henry. "Sometimes dragons are dangerous!"

"I'll be very careful," said Henry's father.

Suddenly Henry's father yelled, "Help, I'm caught!" Then he disappeared from sight.

"Oh dear! What has happened?" gasped
Mrs. Rabbit.

"The dragon has caught him!" cried Henry.

Henry grabbed his wooden sword, and his mother
grabbed a garden fork.

They ran to the bushes . . .

. . . and they found Henry's father caught in the dragon trap.

"Poor dear!" exclaimed Mrs. Rabbit. "What happened to you?"

"Where is the dragon?" asked Henry.

Henry's father didn't want to talk about dragons
any more. "You go to bed right now," he said to Henry.
"And don't get up again!"

Henry went back to his bedroom. He opened his door and he peeked inside.

The dragon shadow was still on the wall.
And something that looked a little like a dragon
was standing near Henry's bed!
Henry raised his sword and he stared at the thing
and he thought, "That dragon looks like . . ."

. . . my cap hanging on the bedpost!"
(Which is exactly what it was.)

Henry wanted to show his parents. So he crept
up behind them, and he made a noise like
rustling bushes.

And he cast the shadow of his cap on the living room wall.

Suddenly Henry's mother looked up at the wall.

"There's a shadow that looks a little like a dragon!" she gasped.

Henry Rabbit started to giggle.
"What an imagination you have!"
he said.